# Willy and Hugh

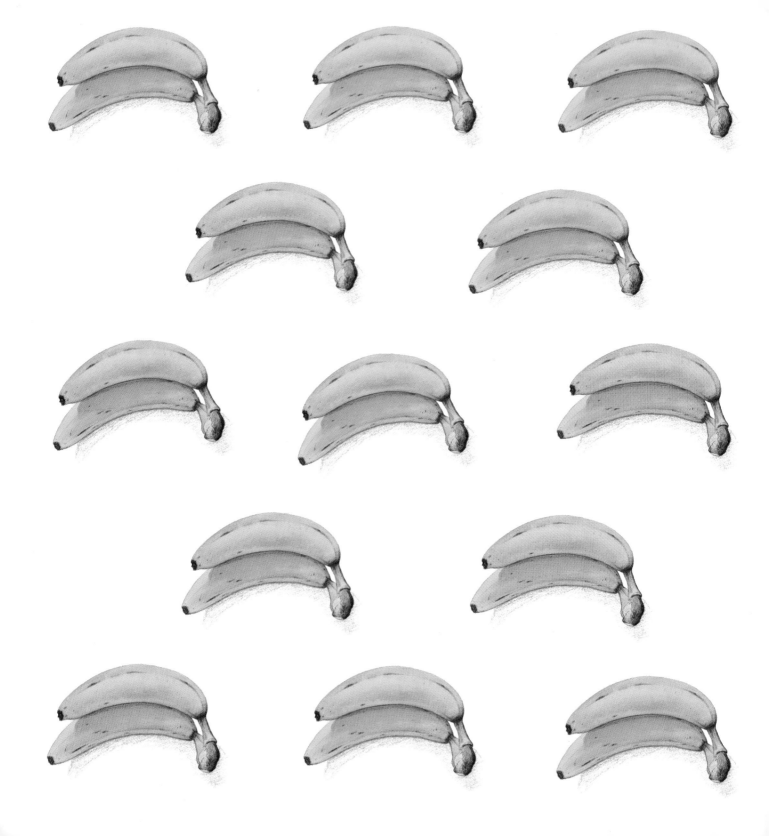

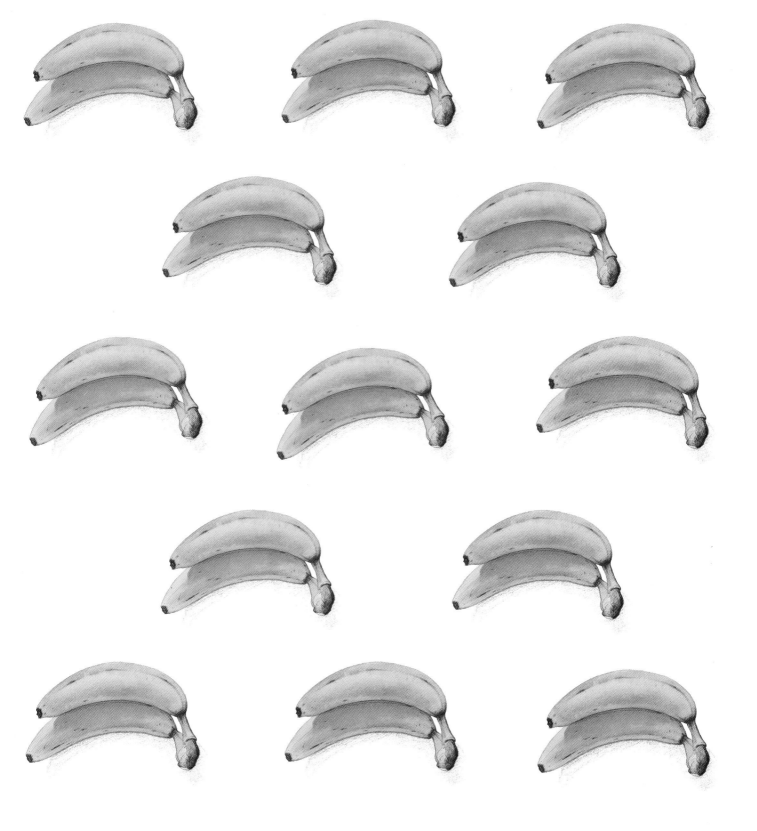

WILLY AND HUGH
A PICTURE CORGI BOOK 978 0 552 55965 2

First published in Great Britain by Julia MacRae

Julia MacRae edition published 1991
Red Fox edition published 1992
Picture Corgi edition published 2008

9 10 8

Copyright © A E T Browne & Partners, 1991

Picture Corgi Books are published by Random House Children's Publishers UK,
61–63 Uxbridge Road, London W5 5SA

www.randomhousechildrens.co.uk

Addresses for companies within The Random House Group Limited can be found at:
www.randomhouse.co.uk/offices.htm

THE RANDOM HOUSE GROUP Limited Reg. No. 954009

A CIP catalogue record for this book is available from the British Library.

Printed in Singapore

# Anthony Browne

# Willy and Hugh

Picture Corgi

Willy was lonely.

Everyone seemed to have friends.
Everyone except Willy.

No-one let him join in any games;
they all said he was useless.

One day Willy was
walking in the park …

minding his own business …

 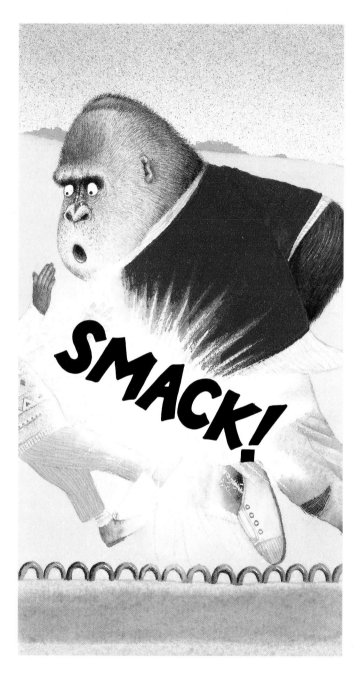

and Hugh Jape was running ...    they met.

"Oh, I'm so sorry," said Hugh.

Willy was amazed. "But *I'm* sorry," he said, "I wasn't watching where I was going."

"No, it was *my* fault," said Hugh. "I wasn't looking where *I* was going. I'm sorry."

Hugh helped Willy to his feet.

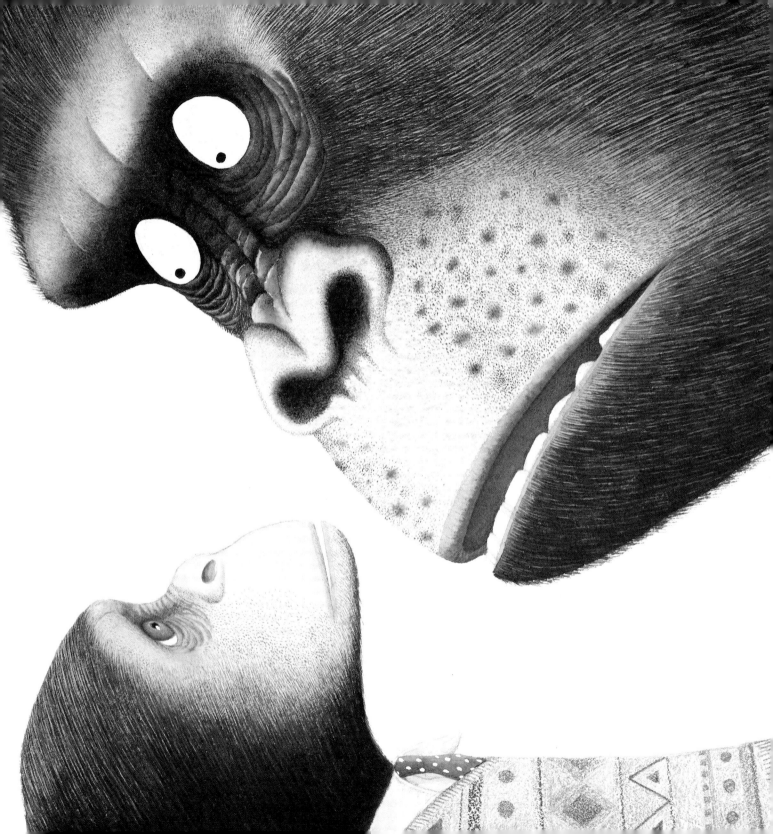

They sat down on a bench
and watched the joggers.
"Looks like they're *really*
enjoying themselves,"
said Hugh.
Willy laughed.

Buster Nose appeared. "I've been looking for you, little wimp," he sneered.

Hugh stood up. "Can *I* be of any help?" he asked.
Buster left. Very quickly.

So Willy and Hugh decided to go to the zoo.

Then they went
to the library, and
Willy read to Hugh.

As they were leaving the library,
Hugh stopped suddenly…

He'd seen a TERRIFYING CREATURE…

"Can *I* be of any help?" asked Willy, and he carefully moved the spider out of the way.

Willy felt quite pleased with himself.

"Shall we meet up tomorrow?" asked Hugh.

"Yes, that would be great," said Willy.

And it was.

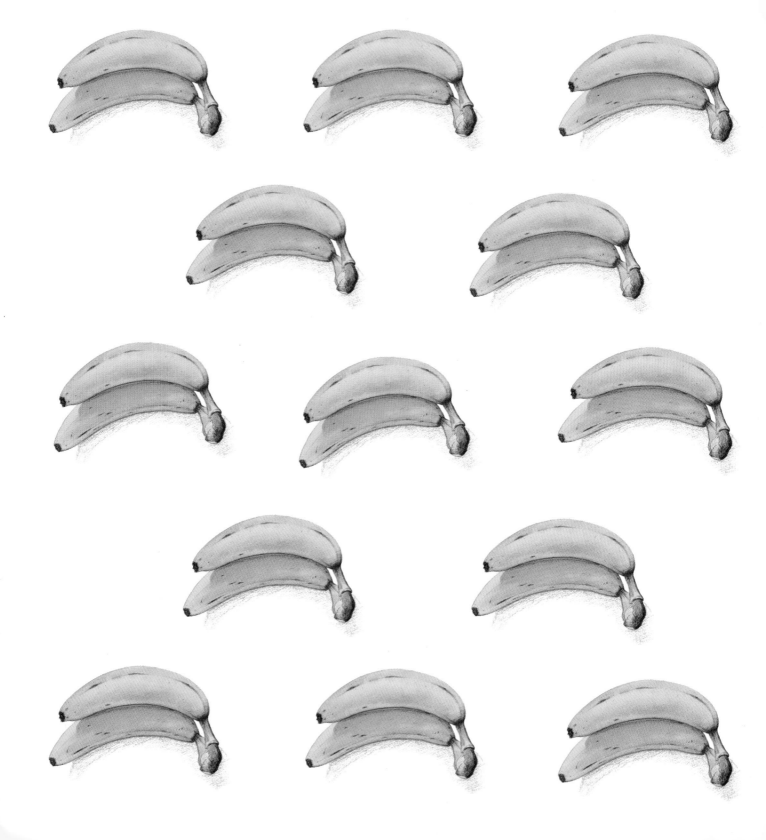

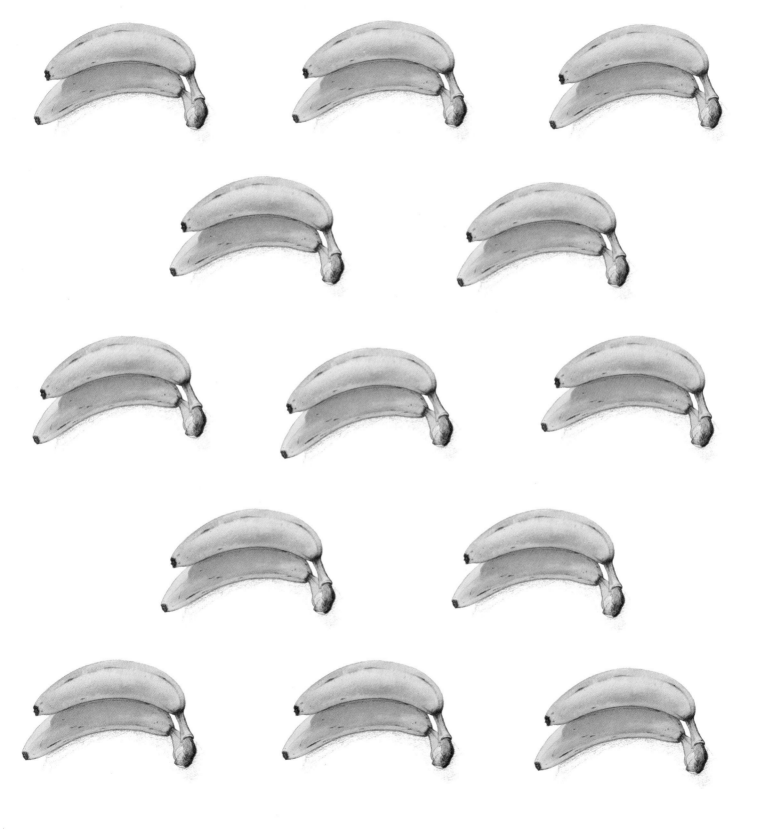

# Anthony Browne

## Read more books starring Willy:

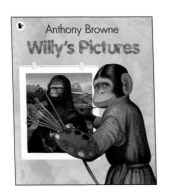
Anthony Browne
Willy's Pictures

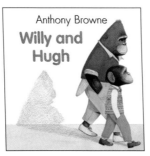
Anthony Browne
Willy and Hugh

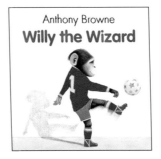
Anthony Browne
Willy the Wizard

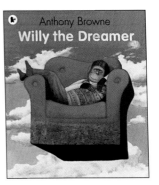
Anthony Browne
Willy the Dreamer

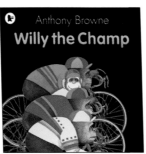
Anthony Browne
Willy the Champ

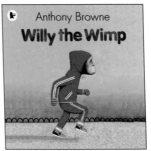
Anthony Browne
Willy the Wimp

## More books by the brilliant Anthony Browne:

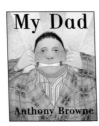
My Dad
Anthony Browne

My Mum
Anthony Browne

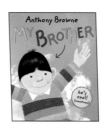
Anthony Browne
My Brother

Voices
IN THE PARK
Anthony Browne

ZOO

THE SHAPE GAME
Anthony Browne

The Night Shimmy

Anthony Browne's
KING KONG